Benny McGee and the SHARK

WE ARE FAMOUS!

For Tom Berhow—the principal at Roosevelt Elementary School who hung my first drawing on his office wall while I was still in kindergarten. This whole journey began with one kind act. I will be forever grateful.

PENGUIN WORKSHOP
An Imprint of Penguin Random House LLC, New York

 Published by Penguin Workshop, an imprint of Penguin Random House LLC, New York. PENGUIN and PENGUIN WORKSHOP are trademarks of Penguin Books Ltd, and the W colophon is a registered trademark of Penguin Random House LLC. Manufactured in China.

Visit us online at www.penguinrandomhouse.com.

Library of Congress Control Number: 2020002192

ISBN 9780593093429 (paperback) 10 9 8 7 6 5 4 3 2 1
ISBN 9780593093412 (library binding) 10 9 8 7 6 5 4 3 2 1

Benny McGee and the SHARK

WE ARE FAMOUS!

by Derek Anderson

Penguin Workshop

CHAPTER ONE

One of my friends at school, Dewey Hill, doesn't believe I know a shark.

But it's true—a great white shark followed me home from the beach.

I let the shark in, gave him ice water, and named him Mr. Chompers.

I even told Dewey how I tried to bring Mr. Chompers to school for my shark report.

He still didn't believe me.

I didn't have a photo of Mr. Chompers, so I drew a picture of us playing together.

It looked just like us.

When I showed Dewey, he said, "That doesn't prove anything! You don't know a shark."

Dewey drives me nuts sometimes.

By the time Mr. Chompers came over to my house after school, I'd forgotten all about Dewey.

I asked my mom to make us fish cookies for a snack.

She didn't want to stink up the house, so she made fish-shaped cookies instead.

I didn't know it then, but those cookies were about to change my life.

CHAPTER TWO

Once the cookies had cooled off, I grabbed a handful.

Mr. Chompers and I dashed off to my room to eat them.

Somehow I tripped on the rug, and the cookies went flying.

Suddenly, there was a lightning-fast flash and a giant chomp.

Not one cookie hit the floor.

"Mr. Chompers . . . did you eat those cookies in *midair*?" I asked.

He stood there, smiling.

"Whoa!" If Dewey Hill didn't believe I knew a shark, he would never believe this.

I had to get it on video.

I grabbed more cookies, borrowed my mom's phone, and made a video. I tossed one cookie after another while Mr. Chompers snatched them out of the air.

I made sure to get myself on camera, too.

Just so I could prove I was there.

The video was perfect.

I asked my mom if I could post it online.

"I guess," she said. But I don't think she was listening.

Now Dewey Hill would know the truth.

After posting the video, Mr. Chompers and I went outside to play.

CHAPTER THREE

When we came back inside, I checked to see if anybody had watched our video.

"That's weird," I said. "Hey, Mom, I think something is wrong with your phone."

"Why?" she asked.

I told her I'd posted the video, and there were two million views.

"Two *WHAT?*" she shrieked. "Let me see that!"

My dad came running. "This can't be right," he said, scratching his head.

My mom and dad watched the video and saw the view count.

It was right.

By dinnertime, there were six million views.

I guess people like to watch videos of sharks doing tricks.

But everything was about to get a whole lot weirder.

CHAPTER FOUR

My mom's and dad's phones began to ring after dinner.

They said the same things to everybody who called.

"Yes, Benny has a great white shark for a friend."

"No, the shark isn't dangerous."

"Yes, he does tricks."

"No, we didn't know about the video."

Then the news stations called.

When their phones finally stopped ringing, my mom and dad made Mr. Chompers and me sit down for a talk.

"Benny, do you have any idea what this means?" asked my dad.

"We are *famous!*" I said. My dad didn't think that was funny.

He said all this attention would be harmful if we let it change us.

What did he know? He wasn't a big star like Mr. Chompers and me.

Nothing was going to change.

Well . . . except for a few fun things, because now we were famous.

COOL

CHAPTER FIVE

The next morning, I put on sunglasses.

Famous people get to wear whatever they want.

I wanted to be cool—you know, for all my fans.

I didn't have sunglasses big enough for Mr. Chompers.

I put my dad's winter scarf on him.

It was hot and scratchy, but he looked cool.

Famous people get to eat whatever they want, too.

So I was surprised there weren't waffles waiting for us when we came down for breakfast.

"Where are the waffles?" I asked my mom.

"There's cereal on the shelf," she said.

"What?" I said. "Do you expect people as famous as Mr. Chompers and me to eat cereal?"

My mom didn't answer. She and my dad were staring out the window.

WITNES
5
9
NEWS 9
PW
NEWS

There were vans from the local TV stations parked up and down our street.

Reporters were everywhere.

"What's going on?" I asked.

"I think they're here to see you and Mr. Chompers," said my dad.

My mom wouldn't let Mr. Chompers and me go outside after that.

She didn't want anybody taking pictures of us. Being famous was like being grounded.

I couldn't go anywhere.
And it was Saturday!

By Sunday, Mr. Chompers and I had to get out of the house.

My mom said we could go with her to the grocery store, but we'd have to wear disguises.

Mr. Chompers and I found a stash of old costumes in the basement. By the time we were finished, you couldn't even tell it was us!

My neighbor, Delaney Gleason, was at the store.

She was looking right at me. I quickly spun around to avoid her.

A woman in curlers was standing right behind me.

"*You,*" she bellowed. "You're that boy from the shark video! Come here. I have *got* to take a picture with you!"

I was so surprised, I backed into an apple display and knocked it over.

My hat and beard fell off.

Apples rolled everywhere while the woman took a picture.

Delaney saw the whole thing.

It was so embarrassing.

CHAPTER SIX

My dad said things were getting out of hand. "Maybe if you do one interview, people will see you're just a normal kid."

He called the *Hello Sunshine Morning Show*. The host, Guy Liberty, is this super-cheerful guy with a big chin.

They said Guy would be at our house the next day.

Guy Liberty and his crew arrived early the next morning.

My mom made me comb my hair and put on a clean shirt.

"Just be yourself," she said. "And don't fidget!"

"Or pick your nose," my dad added.

I didn't know famous people had to follow so many rules!

I told Mr. Chompers to wait in my room. Then I went downstairs to meet Guy.

Guy Liberty's chin was even bigger in person.

He was almost perfect, except for one thing—his tie.

It looked like a fish.

"We thought it would be great for a news story about a shark," Guy explained.

I tried to tell my dad that tie was a bad idea.

"It will be fine," he whispered. "Now go get Mr. Chompers."

It would *not* be fine.

Mr. Chompers is a shark, and that tie looked like a *real* fish.

Then I came up with an idea. My dad had an old winter hat that was way too big.

I grabbed it out of the closet and put it on Mr. Chompers.

It worked. He couldn't see a thing!

I brought Mr. Chompers downstairs.

SHARK
BOOKS
ROCK

Everything was great until a man with headphones said, "The shark can't wear that on TV. Guy will want to see his eyes."

He started counting down. "And we're live in five, four, three, two, one . . ."

I took the hat off Mr. Chompers, and we were on TV!

But the second that Mr. Chompers saw Guy's tie, I knew we were in trouble.

CHAPTER SEVEN

"Good morning, and welcome to our show!" said Guy.

Mr. Chompers was staring, wide-eyed, at Guy's tie.

"No," I whispered. "Don't do it!"

Guy didn't notice. He said, "I know you've seen the shark video by now. I am here with its stars, Benny McGee and a great white—"

Then Mr. Chompers lunged.

I've never heard anyone scream the way Guy Liberty did on live TV.

The lights and cameras went crashing as Mr. Chompers chomped on Guy's fish tie.

I ran to the kitchen to get a cookie.

"Benny," yelled my dad. "This is no time for a snack! Do something!"

But the cookie wasn't for me!

"Hey, Mr. Chompers, look!" I said, tossing the cookie.

Mr. Chompers let go of the tie and went after the cookie.

Then the show went to a commercial break.

We didn't get to finish the interview. Guy Liberty was too shaken up.

My big moment on TV was over.

I always thought if I were famous, my life would be easy—that I wouldn't have any problems. But I was still just the same me, Benny McGee.

CHAPTER EIGHT

My dad was right about being famous—it wasn't much fun.

And it didn't last. The news vans left that afternoon.

Dewey Hill never saw my video.

And he didn't see me on the *Hello Sunshine Morning Show*, either.

He still doesn't believe I have a shark for a friend.

I don't ever want to be famous again.

Who cares if anybody knows who I am, anyway?

Mr. Chompers and I are going to start a big company.

Life will be so easy when we are rich!

About the Author

by Benny McGee

Derek Anderson isn't nearly as famous as Mr. Chompers and me, but he's really good at drawing sharks. Plus, he helps us make our books.

Derek has made a lot of famous books. He made pictures of a duck named Little Quack, a speedy fur ball named Hot Rod Hamster, and Ten Pigs. And he made the pictures *and* stories about Croc and Ally. Mr. Chompers and I like those guys. They're really funny.

Derek writes, draws, and eats cookies in Minneapolis, Minnesota, where he lives with his wife, Cheryl, and their dog, Louie. There's a bunch of cool stuff on his website: www.DerekAnderson.net.

ALSO AVAILABLE:

Benny McGee and the SHARK

THE SHARK REPORT